The Steeple People

Kingdoms Pool

Bobby Days

Best Wishes
Bobby

About the Author

Bobby Days has lived in Combe and the neighbouring village, Stonesfield, all his life, which is where most of the adventures of the Steeple People are set. Bobby has also spent a great deal of time in Cornwall over the years and has built strong relationships in the small seaside town of Mousehole where some of the characters visit from time to time in the series. He has been a Stonesfield Slate Roofer for 35 years and is the main roofer for Blenheim Palace Estates: another setting for our intrepid adventurers! He has had the idea for these novels since his daughter, Shelley, was born in 1990 and finally got round to writing about the adventures of the Steeple People in 2012.

The Steeple People – Kingdoms Pool, is the second in a trilogy of novels about the steeple people family.

The right of Bobby Days to be identified as the author of the work has been asserted by him in accordance with the Copyright, Designs and Patents Act 1988.

ISBN 978-1546444916
first edition

Cover Illustration by Nina Truman
Photographs by Bobby Days

Apart from any use permitted under UK copyright law, this publication may only be reproduced, stored, or transmitted, in any form, or by any means, with prior permission in writing of the publishers or, in the case of reprographic production, in accordance with the terms of licences issued by the Copyright Licensing Agency.

All characters in this publication are fictitious and any resemblance to real persons, living or dead, is purely coincidental.

Printed for Bobby Days in Great Britain by CreateSpace

Copyright © Bobby Days 2017

Thank you

There are many people to thank for their support and encouragement to get the story of The Steeple People told but a few special mentions;

To Shelley, my beautiful daughter of whom I am so proud who inspired me to write this story.

Nina, for your fantastic illustrations. Elena Pearce and Jan Harvey for editing and proofing

Sarah Saunter and the pupils of Stonesfield School, especially Tom Barton, Liam Salter, Catrin Warr, Amber Hands, Ella Thornburn and Edward Martin for your illustrations.

And finally to my wife Vikki, whom I am so proud to have by my side.

Kingdoms Pool

This is a story about some wonderful little people, called The Steeple People, who dwell in the top of the steeple, overlooking Chatterpie Grange in Combelonga, in the Wolds.

A long time ago some people chose to live in houses like you and me, including the people who live in Chatterpie Grange or 'Big 'uns' as they are known to The Steeple People.

Others chose to live underground in the old gold mines and they are known as Fizzlers. And those who made their home in the steeples of the land, were of course known as Steeple People or Steeplers for short.

Bobby Days

The Steeple family is made up of the father, Jack the mother, known as Mam, and their four children, Lulu, Shells Bells and their two brothers, Tiff (short for Christopher) and Joey. They all live in the steeple with their cousins, Buster, Bumble and Bob who are all brothers.

Over the years Steeple People have adapted to living in steeple-sized spaces so they are little people, about 30cm tall. They dress in a similar way to us, eat the same food as us, and laugh and play just like us.

In the summer time this family they move out of the steeple, as it gets very hot up there, and down into the fields below, where they build little houses made out of straw for the whole family to live in until the autumn winds start to blow.

Usually, we can't see or hear Steeplers, but if there is a thunderstorm and the sky is full of electricity you might get a glimpse of them. It's like looking into a river and suddenly you spot a fish, but in a moment it's gone and you wonder if you really did see it or not.

The Steeple People can also do magic. They can shrink things to 'minify' them or 'maxify' them to make them bigger. They do this by holding their noses, pinching their ears, and crossing their legs whilst whistling. It all looks very funny, but it works.

Chapter One

A cold, wet spring made the winter seem even longer, but eventually it turned into the most beautiful summer ever, with white fluffy cottonwool clouds floating around the clear blue skies.

It went on for weeks, occasionally broken by a thunderstorm which helped quench the thirst of the very dry ground.

Buster, Bumble, Bob, Tiff and Joey were camping on the hill overlooking the playing field by the cricket pitch, where on this particular weekend, there was a big white marquee pitched in the middle.

It was the morning after the summer ball and the lads were just waking up. You know that smell when you first wake up in an old tent on a glorious summer morning?

The scent of canvas and crushed grass, well that was exactly what Tiff was smelling right now. Clambering over his crumpled

The Steeple People

sleeping bag he grabbed hold of the zipper at the bottom of the door flap and pulled it right up to the top. Zzzzzzip. Putting the flap to one side and sticking his head out, he took a long sniff. There was a delicious aroma of eggs and bacon being cooked by Buster two tents along.

'Morning Buster,' he called out. 'How are you this beautiful morning?'

'Not bad, mate,' Buster replied, waving with one hand while turning the bacon over with the tongs in his other. 'I was up early, with the crack of sparrows, because I didn't want to miss a moment of this glorious summer's day,' he said grinning. 'And what time did you get to bed last night then?' he asked.

'I can't remember the exact time, but it was very late. I wanted to watch the end of the band playing, weren't they brilliant?'

'Yeah, they were crackin'. What were they called again?' Buster asked, adding more eggs to the pan.

'The Black Diamonds, I think.'

'Oh that's right, Tunnellers group, coal miners they are. I prefer Freefall, much less noisy. Right, it's nearly time to dish up, would you get Bumble and Joey for me please? And make sure they wash their hands.'

'Okay, I'm on my way.' With that Tiff headed off to find them.

Bob had been out collecting firewood in Frogden Spinny for the last hour and was making his way back to camp, when there was a sound he'd never heard before, a whirring, buzzing, clicking sound. Looking round he thought,

'That's not a bumble bee, or even a wasp? It might be a hornet, though, they're larger than the rest.' Just then, right in front of him, he saw it.

'Flippin' 'eck,' he exclaimed, jumping back and dropping the firewood. 'It's a great big Spiderfly. Aarrghh!'

He was absolutely right, it was indeed a Spiderfly. It had just appeared out of Fever Ditch Wood. (Fever Ditch Wood, just so you know, is a dark and mysterious place).

'Aarghh,' he cried again, this time he picked up a stick and held it like a sword. Backing away slowly he started slashing the stick above his head back and forth, back and forth. He knew that if The Spiderfly managed to hover above him, the web it was spinning could be dropped, covering him in a sticky mesh and then the creature could come down and sting him.

'Help!' he called. 'Help! Anybody, please I need some help!'

Chapter Two

Laying in the long grass, Joey was day dreaming about the night before. He hadn't actually gone to bed that night.

He'd stayed up to enjoy the Big 'un's' Summer Ball which had started early the previous evening and finished with a Survivor's Breakfast at dawn. Every year there is a ball with a disco as well as live music. There are also fire-eaters when it gets dark and lots of sumptuous food served on silver plates. There is dancing and singing and everybody from the village joining in the fun.

Joey, thinking about the all the fun they'd had watching the goings on, was lost in his thoughts. Suddenly he heard somebody shouting. Sitting up, and looking around, he saw Tiff clambering over the rickety wooden fence by the oak tree.

'Breakfast is ready Joey.' Tiff called, gesturing him to come over. Getting up, Joey made his way over, dodging the many cowpats on the way. As he climbed the wooden fence at the end of the field, he looked back towards the wood and saw two small figures flying in the sky, a large flying object with a smaller object dangling from its legs, heading towards a clump of trees. 'Hmmm,' he thought, 'that's a bit odd.'

Arriving back at camp both the boys washed their hands before sitting down on the logs surrounding the fire. Buster had already dished up and Bumble was tucking into his breakfast as though he had never seen food before, egg dripping down his chin and on to his shirt.

'Bumble,' Buster cried. 'Slow down, you'll get indigestion if you carry on like that.'

'I'm hungry,' Bumble replied between mouthfuls.

'You're always hungry, Bumble,' said Joey grinning.

'Anyone seen Bob?' asked Buster. They all looked at one another and shrugged their shoulders.

'Wasn't he getting firewood?' asked Tiff, as he scoffed a piece of bacon.

'That's it. I remember now, he said he'd get some first thing before it got too hot. He was hoping he'd spot some wild deer, if he was lucky,' replied Buster.

'Pass the tomato sauce Joey' asked Bumble.

'Of course,' Joey replied and after giving the bottle a good old shake, he threw it straight into Bumble's outstretched hand.

'Good shot, my boy,' he said while taking off the lid and giving the bottom of the bottle a good slap. The sauce came flying out in a gloopy blob, landing on his plate but with the force of the slap, a large globule bounced off his plate, flew through the air, hitting the front of Joey's shorts and some landing on Tiff's face.

'Oi, Bumble,' cried Tiff while wiping the sauce off with his handkerchief.

'Sorry everyone,' Bumble replied mopping up the last of his breakfast from his plate with a hunk of bread. 'Sometimes I forget how strong I am,' then looking towards Tiff he said, 'Can you remember the time when the mill wheel came loose and rolled down the river and smashed into the wall? I rolled it up the hill and fitted it back on, all on my own.'

Unfortunately Joey, who had just taken a big gulp of tea, laughed out loud and ended up spitting his tea out by accident, all over Tiff.

Wiping the tea from his face, Tiff cried, 'Aw, bloomin' 'eck, what next Joey?' Getting

The Steeple People

up quickly he knocked over the cauldron of hot water that was bubbling over the fire.

The water put out the fire and a great big cloud of hissing steam, whooshed up into the air.

'Joey,' he shouted again, 'now look what you've made me do.'

Ella Thornburn age 11

'Oh that's it, blame it on me mate,' Joey said stifling a laugh. 'Sorry it's just Bumble and his daft stories.' Looking at Bumble, he said, 'You dreamt that, you great goose, I remember you telling me about it last year.'

Shaking his head, and looking up at them all, Bumble nodded. 'So I did, you're right. I'm losing my marbles.' Then a big grin split his face in two. 'It would be amazing though, to be that strong, especially as that wheel probably weighs about 10 tonnes, I mean, how could I, a Steepler move that?'

The Steeple People

Amber Hands age 11

Suddenly, Buster cried out, leaping up quickly, 'Look out. Fire! The tent is on fire.'

No-one had noticed that when the cauldron had been knocked over, it had dislodged a log which had rolled out of the camp fire, down the bank and come to rest at the side of Tiff's tent, it had set light to one of the guy ropes which was burning along its whole length. Galloping down the hill, Joey tripped over his shoelace, and losing his footing, he started to roll over towards the burning rope.

'Joey,' Tiff shouted, 'I'm coming.' Tiff launched himself towards Joey, and clasping him in a bear hug they were both suddenly rolling together, until they came to a stop centimetres from the now blazing tent.

Picking up a bucket of water and chasing after them down the hill, Buster threw the water over the tent. With a huge hiss, the flames died down and slowly went out.

'Phew, another close shave,' he gasped.

'I know,' replied Bumble, 'whatever next?' And as soon as he'd said it, Buster accidentally stepped into the empty bucket, staggered backwards and fell head first into the biggest cowpat you have ever seen.

'For goodness sake, what are you like?' Bumble said turning to see Joey and Tiff doubled up with laughter. 'I wish Bob was here, he'd have loved to have seen that.'

And they were right, poor Bob would have loved to have seen it but he was now in a real pickle. Not only had he missed his breakfast, and he loved his breakfast, he was in a very dangerous predicament. In his desperate fight to ward off the Spiderfly, he had stumbled over a log and fallen flat on his back, giving the horrible creature the chance to get close enough to throw a web over him, wrap him up, and then sting him on his bottom!

'Owww! Aargghh, that really hurts you nasty little devil,' he cried, before he passed out.

When Bob came round, he found he couldn't move his arms or legs or breathe properly. Slowly opening his eyes he found he was in total darkness. He didn't know it at the time but after he'd been stung by the Spiderfly it had wrapped him up further in its web, like an Egyptian mummy. Then it had flown him to the dark woods where it had hung him from a tree branch. Hanging there, unable to move his body, he found he could wiggle his head a bit.

Blinking his eyelids and moving his chin, he managed to loosen a bit of the webbing, letting in a tiny chink of light.

The Steeple People

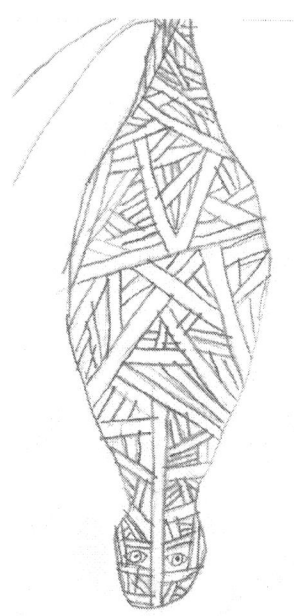

Tom Barton age 11

Through the gap, he could just make out a small white cottage, with a rusty coloured roof nestled down below him and from the chimney of this rickety old building, long wisps of purple smoke curled up towards the tree tops. Tethered next to the picket fence was a rather raggle, taggle old piebald pony with a long plaited mane and a well-worn saddle, drinking deeply, from the stone trough.

'Now that looks like Harry Horsebite to me,' he thought as he struggled to breathe through the small opening. 'So if that's Harry, where's Big Sam?'

Chapter Three

After they had cleared up and Buster had managed to get all the bits of cowpat out of his hair, he turned to them saying,

'Right lads, tomorrow is the annual cricket match between The Combies and The Poachers and I've had an idea. You know last Christmas when we were flying on the birds, coming back from the mill?' They all nodded. 'Well, remember, we got shot at and poor old Bob was hit in the ear with a pellet from one of the guns the poachers use?'

'Yeah,' they said in unison.

'Well, I know Bob wouldn't want us to do anything too bad to get them back, but we could have a bit of fun at their expense.' Buster said with a wink.

'What are you thinking then Buster?' Bumble asked.

'Well, I have a plan but first of all we need to get some bits and pieces together.'

'OK,' said Joey, getting excited, rubbing his hands together. 'What do we need?'

'Lollipop sticks, four balloons, four wicker bread baskets, a potato, some string and last, but not least, some elastic bands,' replied Buster.

The others looked at each other blankly.

'And where on earth are we going to get all that stuff from?' Tiff asked, throwing his hands in the air.

'Come on lads, use your noggin, last night there was a party in the 'Big 'uns' marquee, there's bound to be some balloons left over and maybe some bread baskets. I'm sure we'll find half a potato somewhere. As for the lollipop sticks, why not have a look where the ice cream van was parked?'

'Oh yeah' Tiff replied.

Buster carried on. 'The string should be easy to find as they used loads of it to tie up signs and stuff but the elastic bands...hmmmm, I'm not so sure, your guess is as good as mine but I'm confident you'll come up with something,' he said smiling at them. 'So, quite a lot to do this morning as this afternoon we are off to Fever Ditch Wood to get the last ingredient.'

Pausing to think, he pointed to Tiff and Joey, 'Now you two can go and get the lollipop sticks and keep an eye out for some elastic bands. Good luck. Bumble you can go and find the potato and the baskets and I'll locate some balloons.'

With that they all picked up the things they might need and headed off, in different directions to complete their tasks.

Bumble had made his way to the cricket pavilion and slipped inside through the cat flap in the storeroom door. The room contained all the cricket equipment and was also home to Tildy the tortoiseshell cat, the cricket team's mascot. Checking it was all clear, he started climbing over cricket bats and pads, stumps and the practise netting. It was like an army assault course for him. Eventually he overcame all the obstacles and managed to get to the kitchen door, on the other side of the room.

Looking around he could see that there was a black bag in the kitchen which looked as if it was about to be thrown out as rubbish. After tearing a small hole in the side, he found it was full of waste food from last night's party. Making the tear a bit bigger so he could pull out some of the contents, he saw half cut carrots, onions, and cucumbers. Finally, he spotted a couple of potatoes. 'At last, just what I was after,' he thought to himself, wiping the sweat from his brow. Pulling the potatoes out of the bag he minified them, and then popped them in his jacket pocket.

Scanning the room again, he spotted a cardboard box with all the used plastic plates and cups. Going over for a better look, he couldn't believe it, a stack of bread baskets. He pushed over the stack so they separated and minified three of them.

'What a stroke of luck,' he thought, 'job, done.'

Chapter Four

Buster was at the marquee, checking round every corner and keeping a look out for any quick movements because earlier he'd seen the cat meandering its way up to the playground.

Spotting some deflated balloons on the floor he went over to inspect each one for any holes. He picked the best ones and folded them up like towels to store in his satchel. What he really needed now was the gas to make them float.

As he scrambled up on to a plastic chair, looking around for the gas bottle, he didn't notice Tildy under one of the tables. She was hiding behind the tablecloth with just one eye peeping out, watching his every move.

You see, unlike us, animals can see the Steeplers. He was just about to get off the chair when he heard a faint tinkle of a bell. 'Oh no,' he thought, 'the cat.'

Tildy had a collar with a tiny bell to stop her creeping up on birds. By the time he spotted her beneath him she'd already started to edge forward, watching his every move intently. All she would need to do is take a run and jump and she'd be on the chair next to him in a second and he would be dinner!

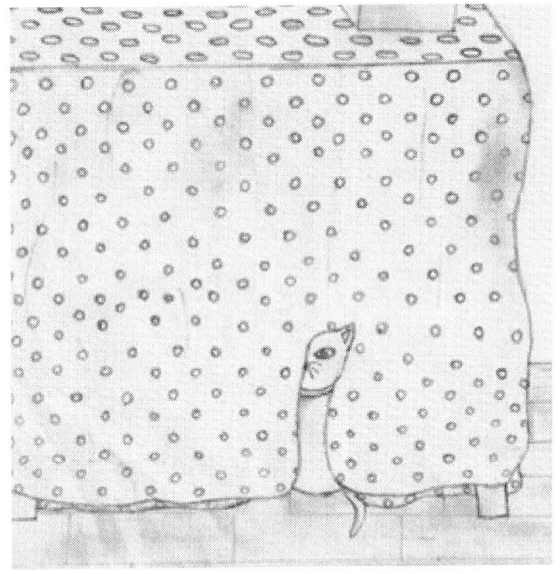

Catrin Warr age 11

Buster had to do something quickly. On the table in front of him was a box full of used napkins.

'Right, nothing to lose.' So with that, he threw himself at the tablecloth, and managing to cling to it, he used all his weight to pull the cloth down one side of the table.

The Steeple People

This moved the box closer to the edge. The cat was still watching his every move. Glancing over his shoulder whilst he was hanging on to the table cloth he could see her shuffling her back legs just like a cheetah, getting ready to pounce. Just as she leapt, Buster gave the cloth one last, hard tug. The box of napkins flew off the table, just as Tildy was mid-leap, completely covering her.

Buster ran right underneath the table, in the direction of the open door as fast as his little legs could carry him. He'd just enough time to clear the doorway and head for the skateboard bowl.

Coming out from under the table cloth, with napkins flying everywhere, the cat caught a glimpse of him disappearing out of the door and within seconds she was right behind him.

Quickly jumping on a roller skate, which must have been accidently left by a child, he scooted down the ramp, lying flat on it, paddling as if he was on a surfboard, heading out to sea. Gaining speed he zoomed down one side of the skateboard bowl to the bottom, then started to go up the other side, not daring to look behind him.

Tildy was hot on his tail, scampering after him. As he neared the rim of the bowl, he jumped off, just as the board went over the top, shooting him right up in the air.

'Wooow – eeeee,' he cried as he flew through the air, then, 'Ouch!' as he landed straight into a mole hill, which fortunately covered him almost completely with soil. The skate landed upside down with the wheels still spinning.

Tildy ran up to the upside down roller skate, gave the wheels a sniff and looked around for Buster. She had lost sight of him as he flew through the air and hadn't worked out where he had landed. After a while she lost interest and started to make her way home, her tail pointing to the sky with indignation.

Buster had kept completely still, having held his breath, so that Tildy wouldn't hear him, but once she was out of sight he pulled himself out of the soil.

Brushing himself off he very hesitantly crept up to the top of the skateboard bowl and after checking the cat had gone, made his way back towards the marquee.

Chapter Five

It didn't take Tiff and Joey long to find the lollipop sticks and after minifying them and storing them in Tiff's pocket, they decided to have a lie down in the shade of a tree because it was quite warm now. Joey had knotted a handkerchief at each corner and put it on his head. When Tiff saw it he burst out laughing.

'What do you look like? You crack me up,' he laughed.

They were looking up through the branches to the sky above and watching the sunlight dance through the leaves, forming a delightful dappled effect on the ground. Joey closed his eyes, enjoying the peace for a moment but just as he started to drift off to sleep, Tiff turned to him and said, 'It'll be Combe Feast tomorrow mate.'

'Yeah,' Joey replied, 'I've been looking forward to that for weeks. The big wheel, the bumper cars, rifle range, the waltzers and the helter-skelter, I can't wait. All transported here in those big lorries,' he said with his eyes still shut. 'I've always wanted one of those Nelly Burgers.'

'What a whole one?' asked Tiff.

'Yep, a sausage, a beef burger, bacon, cheese, onions in a bun and some chips.' he quipped and began laughing out loud.

'It would be the size of your head, mate,' laughed Tiff.

'I know, doesn't it sound good though?'

Suddenly it started to feel cooler, squinting out of one eye, Joey looked up to see a big, dark cloud edging over the sun.

'Reckon we're gonna get some rain mate,' he said, and with that the first raindrops plopped on his forehead.

Getting up quickly, they ran up the bank towards the trunk of the tree, which would give them better cover from the rain. Suddenly the heavens opened and the rain came pouring down and then turned into hailstones.

'Thank goodness that we we're here Joey,' wheezed Tiff, who was slightly out of breath from the quick dash, or else we'd be goners.' Of course, to us the hail was the size of marbles but to the Steeplers the hailstones were the size of tennis balls, can you imagine it?

The storm lasted a good ten minutes or so and by then they were very awake and raring to go to find the elastic bands.

Tiff turned to Joey and asked, 'Where do you think we can get the elastic bands from?'

'I haven't got a clue,' he said shrugging his shoulders. 'Let's have a think, now, who would have elastic bands?' He paused for a moment. 'I know,' he exclaimed, 'they sell them at the Post Office, don't they?'

'Umm.. you're right, but we've got no way of buying things from a 'Big 'uns' shop,' reasoned Tiff.

They both sat looking out at the raindrops dripping from the branches of the old tree wondering what to do.

Then Tiff blurted out, 'Of course, the post lady, the post lady always carries elastic bands to wrap up piles of letters.'

'Yes she does but we can hardly walk up to her ask for some can we?'

'Hang on a minute, what time is it?' Tiff asked.

'Five and twenty minutes past twelve.'

'And what time is the post collection?' asked Tiff.

'Five and twenty minutes to the hour.' Joey answered, grinning as he realised what his brother was getting at.

'OK, let's get a move on and make our way to the post box,' said Tiff, 'we've only got ten minutes.'

With that they picked up their belongings and headed for the post box. It was hard going for the little chaps trudging through the wet grass to the playground. By the time they got there they only had a few minutes to spare.

After clambering over the dry stone wall, they made their way towards the church. Approaching the bottom of Parsons Hill, they couldn't miss the presence of the huge cedar tree that towered over a red telephone box beneath it.

Around the corner of the little gravel lane they came upon the post office with its newly thatched roof. Settling down on the bank, Joey said,

'Let's wait for a moment, we have a good view from here.'

'Ok mate,' he replied, 'good idea, you can look that way and I'll look up the road, this way.'

The sun had come back out and it was warming up again, steam started to lift from the ground as the rain dried in the heat.

After a while, they heard tyres crunching on the gravel, as the little red van post van approached. Pulling up opposite the post box, the post lady got out of the van and made her way over to it. She opened it up and started to take out all the letters that had been posted that day, bundling them into tidy packs to go in her grey post bag. Getting a ball of elastic bands out of her pocket she took a couple off it, and started to put them round the pile of envelopes in her hand.

Joey elbowed Tiff in the side, winked at him, then made his way over to the post box.

Suddenly the post lady felt a tug on the bottom of her trouser leg, quickly followed by the barking and growling of a dog,

(Joey was very good at animal sounds.) Instantly, she jumped back and dropped the envelopes and the ball of elastic bands, which started bouncing down the lane. Tiff was

The Steeple People

watching all this from under the cedar tree, crying with laughter.

Looking round the post lady realised there was no dog and feeling rather confused, the she went back towards the box. Hurriedly picking up the rest of the letters and looking out for the dog she could have sworn was tugging her leg, she locked the box, made her way back to the van and drove off.

The ball of elastic bands had come to a stop by a big stone. Tiff minified it, and it was now the size of a football to him, so he carried it under his arm.

'That was genius Joey, just brilliant,' he was still chuckling, and shaking his head.
'I know mate, you should've seen her face. She'll be wondering what all that was about for the rest of the day!

Chapter Six

Tiff and Joey decided to go back to the camp via the churchyard, which was a lovely walk. Squeezing through the gaps in the church gate, they looked up at the church steeple and on the big blue clock face they noticed that instead of having 12, 3 6 and 9 around the edge it had 1, 4 8 and 9.

'Well, there's a thing Joey, that's the first time I've noticed those numbers on the clock,' said Tiff.

'Me too,' he replied. 'That's probably why they call it Silly Combe.' They burst out laughing again.

'Oh I don't know,' chuckled Joey, while plucking a blade of grass, examining it and then putting it in the corner of his mouth.

'Dad told me about someone putting a pig on the wall to watch the band go by. They dressed it up in trousers, a shirt, a yellow waistcoat and a big red hat on its head.'

Tiff looked at him astonished 'Really? I bet it looked a pretty picture,' he said with a grin, and at the same time he grabbed the piece of grass protruding from Joey's mouth.

'Oi you,' Joey protested grabbing hold of Tiff. He was trying to get him into a headlock, which made them both lose their balance and fall over. Tiff dropped the elastic band ball he was holding and it started to roll and bump down the gravel path towards the gate. At the very same time coming round the corner of the church, was Mungo the highland terrier. He was sniffing each gravestone as he made his way towards them. He immediately spotted the ball of elastic bands bouncing down the path and instinctively ran towards it.

'NOOOOOOO!' the boys shouted together.

'Not that dog again,' cried Tiff.

'How the flippin' heck are we going to get it back now,' sighed Joey, kicking a stone and stubbing his toe.

'Oww.' He hopped over to the bank to sit down, threw off his shoe and started to rub his toes.

Tiff, taking no notice of all this, crouched down and with his thumb and forefinger rubbed his chin, deep in thought.

He was remembering the time at Christmas, when Mungo chased Buster and Bumble across the Great Hall back at The Grange, at the Big 'uns' Christmas Ball. He had very nearly caught them and it would have been curtains for them both if it hadn't been for his Dad's quick thinking to get them all through the trap door. Ever since then, the family had been very wary of that dog.

'What are we going to do Tiff? Joey asked, still rubbing his toe.

'Sshhh. Let me think,' replied Tiff.

Chapter Seven

The dog was having great fun, slobbering all over the tiny ball, holding it between his paws, trying to chew it but it would spring back to shape in his mouth and he'd lose grip on it, making it roll away, so the daft dog would chase after it again. Finally he lost grip on it one last time and the ball hit a stone and began to bounce along the downward sloping path, rolling right under the church gates.

Mungo chased it but was cut off by the gates so ended up sitting there, looking at the ball longingly and whimpering as if he'd just lost his best friend. Tiff was watching all this and had seen where the ball had rolled.

'Joey,' he whispered, because a dog has very good hearing and he didn't want them to be spotted. 'I've got an idea how to get past Mungo and get our ball back.'

'How?' asked Joey, still sulking slightly over his sore toe.

'Right, now, listen. It's a long shot but if we can locate the zip wire attached to the top of the steeple that runs down to the old water pump outside the post office, we might have a chance to get over the gate without the dog catching us.'

'Now, slow down,' Joey replied, 'zip wire? What zip wire?' Joey was puzzled.

Tiff put a finger to his lips, and whispered, 'The Combe Steeplers who lived there had a zip wire installed so they could move freely to and from the church steeple, even if there was a congregation attending a service. They used it to escape from the fire,' he replied.

'Fire? What Fire?' Joey raised his eyebrows. 'I don't know anything about a fire.'

'That's another of Bumble's stories. You mean you've never heard it? He told it one night when we were sitting round the camp fire and a spark flew out. He said we should all be aware of the dangers of fire because something as simple as a candle being too close to a curtain started that one in the tower. It spread quickly too, right to where the family were sleeping.'

Joey gave the tower another glance.

'The father of the family, Big Tone, got them all out by using the zip wire, one by one. He had to wind the handle after each person went down. He was the last one to leave. Thankfully they all managed to escape safely and reach the ground.'

'So what happened to them, because no-one lives in that steeple now?'

'Well, some say they lodged with the Fizzlers for a bit, living in those underground mines but they didn't stay for long because they got a bit claustrophobic and then after that no one knows.'

'What a sorry tale,' said Joey.

Tiff and Joey quickly made their way to the door on the shaded side of the church. Squeezing through a crack at the bottom, they found themselves in a little room with a small fireplace on one side and an ornate glass window on the other. Moving across the room they went into the main part of the church through a big arched doorway.

'Wow.' Joe sighed as he looked around and saw the coloured beams of light from the stained glass windows, dancing upon the walls and floor. It was a beautiful old building. They both took a moment to take in the beauty of the church, staring up at the murals and the stained glass and enjoying the peace and quiet.

'Come on, we've got to find the way up to the top of the tower,' said Tiff and with that he disappeared behind a heavy, dark red curtain and Joey quickly followed.

Outside Mungo, was getting more and more frustrated scrabbling with his front paws under the big oak gate, yelping and barking and getting himself into a right old state. The chime of the church bell rang, then again, and again and again. Looking up towards the noise, Mungo cocked his head to one side. He was responding to his name being called. From the top of the tower, there were two tiny little people waving and shouting. Cocking his head to the other side, as if trying to understand, he started yapping and barking, as though he was trying to tell them off for calling to him.

Suddenly there was a whirring sound and a high pitched 'PING' followed by a whining, whirring noise. The boys had not only got to the top of the tower but they had managed to find the handle for the zip wire, pull it tight and were heading down it flying towards Mungo and the gate.

'Na, Na, Nee Na Na,' Joey called out as they flew over the dog, while Tiff stuck his tongue out at him. They went straight over the top of the gate, landing with a thump at the bottom of the wire by the old water pump.

Jumping up, Tiff ran over to where he thought the ball of elastic bands had rolled. After hunting about for a minute or two he found it, wiped the dog slobber off using the cuff of his shirt and carrying the ball under his arm, he turned to poke his tongue out at Mungo.

Unfortunately for them, the more they goaded the little dog the more determined it made him to get to them. Running the length of the gate from side to side Mungo was getting more and more angry. Sniffing about he found a small hole in the bottom of the wooden panel to the side of the gate and managed to get his head through. He wiggled and wiggled his little body until he managed to squeeze through the tiny gap completely. As soon as he was free from the fence he darted towards the boys.

Looking over his shoulder Joey saw the dog was after them and was gaining fast.

'Tiff,' he cried, his laughter turning in to a shriek of panic 'Oh no, that dog is like a missile, quick, run!'

Tiff didn't look round he just started running towards the playground. Dropping the ball of elastic bands he was still carrying, he jumped up and caught hold of the swing. Pulling himself up on to the seat, and kneeling down, he grabbed the chain in one hand and put his arm out for Joey. Mungo was just feet away, gnashing his teeth. Tiff was trying to pull Joey up but the weight on the swing made it move and gave Mungo the opportunity to leap up and catch hold of the bottom of Joey's trousers.

'Arrgghhh, he's got me trousers, pull me up Tiff', shrieked Joey.

Mungo tightened his grip on poor old Joey's trousers and shook his head. Joey thought his trousers were going to be ripped off. Mungo was shaking Joey so hard the lad's teeth were clattering.

'H-H- Hee-..ll-ll….pp me Tiff-ff-ff, I'm g-g-g-g-going to be s-s-s-sick if he shakes me any ha-ha-harder.'
Suddenly in the distance they heard,
'Mungo. Oh Mungo. Where are you? Come on boy, its dinner time'
Then they heard what sounded like a spoon being hit against a metal bowl. Immediately the little angry dog released his

grip on Joey's trousers and ran off back towards his owner.

'Oh my giddy aunt, I thought you were a gonner then Joey.' Said Tiff as he let go of his brother's arm and let him drop to the floor.

Instantly dropping to his knees and panting Joey didn't say anything he just gulped air and looked very pale.

Once Joey had turned back to his normal colour and was feeling better they gathered up the ball and their other belongings and started to walk back to the camp.

Chapter Eight

At last, nearly everyone had returned to camp after their adventures. They'd all manged to find the bits and pieces they needed so settled down for a well-earned sandwich. The first thing they did when they finished lunch was to maxify the bread baskets and repair any holes in them with string. Buster maxified the two lollipop sticks, put them together to form a cross and used a brass hook, which he had brought from home, to secure them through the centre to make a propeller. (He always came prepared.) Joey brought the potatoes to Buster and asked what they needed them for.

'The spud guns,' Buster replied with a smile, 'just for protection. You see my boy, where we're going later, we may well need them.'

'Oh,' Joey said looking worried.

'It's a dangerous place, is Fever Ditch Wood.'

Joey shivered 'Oh golly.' He murmured to himself.

Tiff and Bumble had been busy attaching two balloons to each bread basket.

'Now Tiff, if you would hold the necks of the balloons open, then I'll fill them with this gas'. Buster called. He had found a small gas bottle at the marquee minified it and brought it back. Once the balloons were floating in the air, he tethered each basket to the next to form a row, like carriages of a train. The last job was to fit the lollipop stick propellers to the front of the first basket then secure the elastic bands to drive the propellers.

When they had finished they all went over to the fire and had a nice cup of tea and admired their handywork.

Chapter Nine

Bumble was on his way back to the camp from visiting the thunderbox (toilet to you and me) when he heard the sound of a horse approaching from behind. Turning around he saw it was Big Sam on his old horse, Harry, who came to a halt just in front of him. Bumble looked up at Big Sam.

'Are you alright then Sam?' Bumble asked.

'No, I mean yes. I'm OK, but poor old Bob isn't,' Sam replied.

'Eh? What do you mean, Bob isn't?' Jumping down from the horse, Sam looked at Bumble with concern.

'I have just visited Wolfstun the Wuzard at his potion house, by Kingdom's Pool in Fever Ditch Wood,' he explained slowly. 'Something caught my eye out of the window, and I saw a nasty old Spiderfly landing on a branch of the old cedar tree. It had a bundle hanging below on its silk threads. After securing it to the tree, it flew off deeper into the wood, the bundle was left hanging there.'

'Why are you telling me all this and what has it got to do with Bob?'

'I'm sorry to say it but that bundle was Bob.'

'What? But how do you know that for sure?' Bumble felt his heartbeat quicken. 'It could have been an animal or something else.'

'Well, if that animal had hobnail boots on and a red and black checked shirt then I suppose it could be,' Sam replied.

'Oh, no.' Bumble's bottom lip started to quiver. 'That's what Bob was wearing this morning. Oh Sam,' he sobbed. 'What are we going to do now?'

Sam put his big arms around Bumble's shoulders, he could see that Bumble was about to cry.

'Come on, come on, pull yourself together mate. We've got to go and rescue him.' And with that, he took Bumble's little face in his big, rough, hands and rubbed away a stray tear with his thumbs, like you would to your own brother to make him feel better. 'Come on, let's go and find the rest of the gang and then together we can come up with a plan.' He hoisted Bumble onto Harry's back and began to lead the horse by the reins into camp.

Buster looked up from inspecting the baskets for the flight, and was surprised to see Bumble on the back of a horse being led by Big Sam.

'Well, hello Sam,' he called, 'what's Bumble been up to this time?'

'Hello Buster,' said Sam. 'Bumble's not been up to anything, but we've got a problem somewhere else.'

Joe and Tiff had joined them. Sam lifted Bumble down from the horse and Buster could tell Bumble wasn't his usual self.

'You alright boy?'

'No it's awful.' Bumble replied glumly, looking down at the ground.

'What's up? tell me,' asked Buster

Then it all came tumbling out at once as Bumble tried to explain.

'Bob's been captured by one of those Spiderflies and taken to Fever Ditch Wood, and wrapped up in a web. I don't know if he's alive or dead, we need to go to him now.'

With that, Tiff, Joe and Buster burst out laughing. 'That's a good one,' said Joe. 'Your stories are getting more and more far-fetched every time.'

'He has, he actually has,' Bumble cried out, his eyes filling up with tears again.

'He's telling the truth Buster,' said Sam, 'I saw it happen.' Sam tethered Harry to the fence. Suddenly the laughter stopped and they all looked at Sam and waited for him to continue.

'I saw Bob tied up there about two hours ago. I'm just sorry I couldn't help him at the time.'

The Steeple People

Everyone stood stunned for a moment and then Buster said, 'Gosh, we're going to have to go and get him. Right, boys, sit down on those logs. I have to tell you about Fever Ditch Wood and then we have to come up with a plan to get Bob home.'

Chapter Ten

Fever Ditch Wood is a very dangerous place, somewhere only the most intrepid of people would dare to go. Buster was explaining this to Joe and Tiff, whilst Bumble was wringing his hands. Big Sam was drinking a cup of tea from his flask and listening intently.

'Now, I know I said we were going to have an adventure, but this is no longer a bit of fun, this is now deadly serious.' Bumble said, looking at each of them gravely. 'I'm going to try to prepare you for the perils you may face while we're in there. For example, there are some very odd creatures that live there that you'll never have come across them anywhere else, I can tell you. There are Tygons for a start. They are fire-breathing beasts with the front half of a tiger and the back tail of a dragon. Then we will probably see Blowpines, they are similar to a porcupine, but with a mouth like a blowpipe. A Blowpine will shoot its quills out and they are deadly accurate. Of course, you already know about the Spiderflies, they spin sticky webs as they fly which they drop on their prey before swooping down to sting them. Horrible.'

'That's not what's happened to Bob is it?' Joey asked, looking at Tiff in horror.

Buster nodded his head.

'It sounds like it Joe, but don't worry, the sting only stuns the victim.' Trying to hide the fear in his voice, he continued, 'there are also Glowpigs, which glow red when they are disturbed and puff themselves up to produce spikes out of their backs.'

Tiff piped up, 'Buster, with all these deadly things in Fever Ditch Wood, how are we going to protect ourselves, if they attack us?'

'I'll come to that in a moment, but please don't interrupt Tiff, I've got so much more to tell you before we can get going. Now, last but not least, the Decapus.'

'The Decapus!' both boys said together.

'Yes,' said Buster looking at them as if to say, I just told you not to interrupt, 'the Decapus. The closest thing you would know to it is an octopus which as you know has eight legs, but a Decapus has ten. It hides up in the tree tops and changes colour to blend in with whatever it is clinging to, the perfect camouflage.'

'Oh, my giddy Aunt.' Joey blurted out. 'Please, Buster, what have we got to protect ourselves?' Will a spud gun really be any good?'

'I have, with your Dad, Jack's blessing, brought with me the Rhombus Spectrum,' replied Buster.

Sam who up until now had been sitting quietly drinking his tea, coughed rather loudly, 'Ahem.'

With that Buster bent down, rummaged through his rucksack and pulled out a small wooden box with an embossed elephant design on its lid.

Holding it tightly in his hands he turned to Sam and explained, 'This is our Rhombus Spectrum, the guardian of us all, our defence and our shield.'

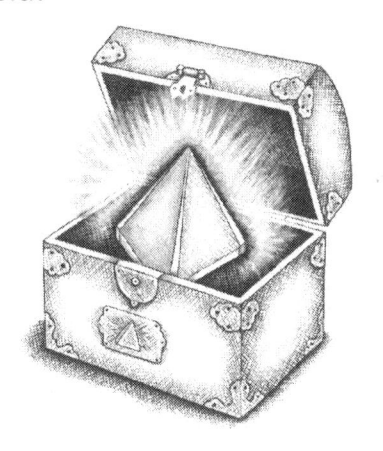

'I had heard such a crystal existed,' said Sam, 'and I'd heard the rumour that the Queen of Snowland had bestowed such an item upon some of her subjects, but I had no idea it was the Steeple People.'

'Yes, we were given it when the Snow Circus came last year,' said Bumble proudly.
'But obviously it's a very special thing, so we don't go blurting it out to everyone that we've got one. A long time ago, one of our ancestors did a good deed for the Royal family and this is how the Queen repaid us. With your help and knowledge of the wood Sam, we can rescue Bob and if he's injured the crystal will help heal him. We must all remember that the powers, even though they are special, cannot bring people back to life,' he said with urgency in his voice.

'Of course I will help you,' said Sam.

Buster turned back to the rest of them. 'Right, now we need to get going. We'll need some ropes, the net, any camping knives, spud guns and a big wodge of luck.'

Chapter Eleven

As they headed down the field towards Fever Ditch Wood, Buster explained what he'd wanted to do with the airships they'd built earlier. He told them he had wanted to fly over the cricket field and drop itching powder on the Poachers who would be playing cricket below. He realised they all needed cheering up and said, 'Our plans have changed now, so when we get back after rescuing Bob, we'll use the airships to fly over Combe Feast.' That made them all smile.

Entering the wood, it felt clammy, rather like being in a big greenhouse full of exotic plants, it also had a musty smell. They all wrinkled up their noses. Harry and Sam led the way with the rest following in single file, trailing in the horse's footsteps. They had only been walking ten minutes, when Sam held up his hand drew Harry to a standstill.

Putting his finger to his mouth he turned and whispered.

'I can hear something.' They all listened intently.

They could indeed hear something in the distance, it was like a whimpering sound of a creature in pain.

Jumping down from Harry, Sam gave the reins to Buster and slowly picked his way through the undergrowth. After some yards he came to a mound of dark earth. He got the feeling that there was something behind it so he crept stealthily and peeped over the top.

There, not feet away from him, was a scruffy looking creature. It was lying down licking its paw which had a tiny spear in it. Rubbing his eyes, Sam muttered to himself, 'Blimey, that's a Tygon.'

It was, as Buster had explained earlier, a tiger mixed in with a dragon, and there it was lying down, licking a wound on its paw. Sam was in a very dangerous position. He was only metres away from a wild animal, and worse, an animal in pain. He began to back away, retracing his steps back to the group.

'I've just seen a Tygon and its wounded which means it's dangerous,' he told them. 'We need to get out of here as quietly as we can.'

'Oh no,' Bumble said, 'we can't leave it in pain, we have to help the poor animal.'

Joey stared at him in disbelief. 'Help a ferocious animal that is just as likely to gobble us all up?' Moving closer and putting his hand on Joey's arm, Bumble explained that no animal, beast, human or Steepler should be left to suffer.

'We all have a responsibility and duty to help those in vulnerable situations, or who are worse off than ourselves,' Bumble said.

'I know that but it's so dangerous and my tummy is tying itself up in knots already. I'm frightened, it would be madness to help it.' Tiff put his arm around his brother's shoulder, pulling him close.

'Bruv, now look, unfortunately we have very little choice here. The truth is this beast lies directly in our path and we need to rescue poor Bob. So we have to do something, and do you know, Bumble's right, we can't let it suffer.'

Pointing at Sam, Buster spoke up. 'You know, Sam is very kind to animals, a sort of 'whisperer', he knows a thing or two about them and how they behave. Some say he can almost talk their language and communicate with them in a way we don't understand. Can't you Sam?'

Looking bashful, Sam turned and stroked Harry's head,

'I suppose you could put it like that,' he replied. 'I do talk to them but I've never tried to talk to one of those wild beasts.' Pausing to think, and then with a little more confidence, he said 'I'll give it a go.'

Chapter Twelve

Making their way towards the Tygon who was still whimpering, they suddenly got the feeling they were being watched.
(Do you ever get that creepy feeling?)

Arriving at the mound, they let Sam go up first and then followed. The poor animal had turned around into a tight ball and had its back to them with its red tail curled around itself.

Sam whispered, 'Golly that's a bit of luck, he can't see us. Now we've got to be dead quiet. Bumble give me the bag with the net in it please, and Buster, I need the ropes.'

Perching just below the ridge of the mound, Sam unravelled the net, then tied the ropes to the four corners, securing each with a slip knot. He whispered, 'Right everybody, we've got to act fast, each of you hold on to a piece of rope and I'll carry the net. When I say 'go' we'll run over to the beast and I'll throw the net over it. You guys run round and pull the ropes tight, OK? But only after I say 'go'.

They all climbed to the top of the mound and sat with their little hearts pumping away and their mouths dry as toast.

'Go!' shouted Sam and, with that, he threw the net and the Steeplers ran round the Tygon.

With a mighty roar the Tygon twisted around and its long red tail lashed out from under the net, smacking Tiff round his legs.

'Owww!' Tiff called out in pain, but he didn't let go of the rope, in fact he held it even tighter.

'Pull,' yelled Sam, 'pull lads with all your might.'

The Steeple People

The Tygon was now lashing out at each of them, trying to rip the net with its jaws, frothing at the mouth and letting out puffs of grey smoke.

Sam positioned himself right by its head and looked the beast right in the eye. He then started making a deep throaty purring sound. The Tygon slowly stopped fighting, Sam purred again, this time with a sort of rhythm to it.

The Tygon looked back at him, putting his head to one side. Sam continued to make the purring sound. After a few moments the beast had quietened down. Sam took the opportunity to look at the spike in the poor creature's paw. Still purring and now making a chuffing sound too, he slowly put his hand through the holes in the net and stroked the gold and black striped front leg. Slowly stroking his way down to the paw, he realised he had seen one of these spikes before. 'My goodness' he thought, 'if I'm not mistaken that is the quill of a Blowpine and there is only one way to get it out.'

Looking over to the rest of the gang, Sam motioned for them to loosen the ropes a bit to give him more room to manoeuvre. He could see that the poor animal was totally exhausted and very weak. Gently he grasped hold of the quill with both hands and pulled it with a clockwise twist movement and low and behold, out it came, leaving the Tygon lying there panting with little smoke rings coming from its nose.

Turning to Buster, Sam asked, 'Does the crystal work on animals too?'

Shrugging his shoulders Buster replied,

'I don't know but we might as we'll give it a go.'

They slowly removed the netting from the now motionless creature. Buster passed the small casket to Sam telling him the secret combination to open it. Placing it on the muddy ground right next to the Tygon, Sam said the magic words 'Rhombus Spectrum' and, slowly, the lid of the casket opened.

'Here we go,' he said backing away from the self-opening lid. A bright light shone from inside the little box, the more the lid rose the brighter it became, until they all had to shield their eyes from the dazzling white brightness surrounding them. Slowly a bubble started to form around the Tygon, totally engulfing it. Then, just as when you shake a snow globe and all the glitter and snowflakes swirl around, flecks of gold started sparkling inside the bubble and finally a flash of lightning. After what seemed like ages, but was probably only a minute, the glitter settled and the Tygon was left sitting up, with what looked like a smile on its face.

Then 'Pop!' the bubble burst and the lid to the little casket slammed shut. They couldn't believe their eyes. What was only a few moments ago, a bedraggled looking creature, with a dull, scaly tail, was now a perky, freshly-cleaned animal with a gleaming black and gold striped coat and a red tail that shone like highly polished leather. Its attitude seemed much improved too.

They didn't know what to do now. In fact they were in an even worse position than they were before, because now the animal was strong again and seemingly in no discomfort, so it could quite easily attack all of them. Joe's tummy went into a knot and his legs turned to jelly. You know that ache you get when you're really frightened, he was feeling that right then. Standing up, the animal turned and faced all of them one by one, winking at each of them in turn, then gave a little bow.

They all relaxed a little, although instinct told them to still be alert, but the truth was they thought that they could see in the Tygon's eyes that it was grateful to them for their help. Tiff glanced at Joey and smiled. Suddenly they felt less afraid.

The Tygon turned to Sam and made another chuffing sound. Sam chuffed back. When Sam had finished, he bowed his head.

'His name is Terry,' he said.

Chapter Thirteen

After watching Terry disappear back into the gloomy wood, they gathered their things and continued on their quest to rescue poor Bob. Sam was leading Harry, clearing a path for the Steeplers through the brambles, roots and fallen branches. Suddenly Harry stopped dead in his tracks with his ears twitching back and forth and then without warning broke free of Sam's grip and shot through the bushes in a completely different direction.

Sam, knowing Harry well, quickly realised that he had been alarmed by something that was going to put them in immediate danger.

'Quick, after him,' Sam hollered, as he vaulted over a branch, heading in the same direction as Harry, towards a big old tree trunk that looked as though it had lain on its side for years and was covered in moss.

Zip. Thwack. Zip. Thwack, they heard the sound of Blowpine quills flying through the air and hitting the trees around them.

'Quickly,' Sam shouted, throwing himself behind the log. Harry was hiding a short distance away in some bushes, his ears still twitching.

One by one the Steeplers found shelter behind the log with Sam. Zip. Thwack. Zip, Zip. Thwack. Thwack. They could hear those deadly quills trying to find them.

'What are we going to do, Sam?' asked a very frightened Joey.

'We can't stay here and that's a cert'.' Sam replied, taking a quick look around.

'Tiff, did you bring the walkie-talkie with you by any chance?' asked Buster.

Rummaging about in his bag, Tiff's found the walkie-talkie right at the very bottom. 'Yes, here it is,' he replied passing it over to Buster.

Zip. Thwack. Zip. Thwack. They were well and truly under attack and stuck behind the huge log, surrounded by the vicious Blowpines.

Buster pressed the emergency button on the handset of the walkie-talkie and it instantly sent an alarm sound back to the base station unit, over at the Steeple.

Buster quickly reached into his bag and withdrew the casket with the Rhombus Spectrum. Activating it, once again the bright light shone out from the box and the dome bubble that had previously covered Terry the Tygon began to form all around the Steeplers, Sam and even Harry.

The Steeple People

Zip. Thud. Zip. Thud. The quills were now hitting the bubble and bouncing off but they were still completely surrounded by at least fifteen of the nasty Blowpines, all firing at will.

'Phew, that was close,' said Joey, brushing his hair out of his eyes with the back of his trembling hand. Bumble had managed to get through to Mam on the walkie-talkie.

'Hiya, Mam. We're in a bit of a pickle at the moment,' said Bumble. Don't worry the boys are OK.' He tried to keep his voice calm as he knew how much she'd panic. 'I was wondering if you could get Jack on the line.'

Chapter Fourteen

Bob was watching intently from his lofty position hanging from the tree branch, at the goings on at the little cottage below him. He could see several Glow Pigs snuffling around outside and an old man in robes poking at the remains of a bonfire with a shovel. It looked as if he was trying to flick something out of it.

Bob watched him use the shovel to take what looked like a bottle inside the cottage. He could see him through the open doorway and watched him tip the contents of the bottle into a large cauldron.

All of a sudden, there was a blinding flash of light and a thunderous bang which made all the windows of the cottage shake.

The old man was thrown back outside, through the doorway, which sent the Glow Pigs into full panic mode. They began running around in circles, snorting and squealing. They were now gleaming bright red, with little thorn-like spikes protruding from their backs. They had been frightened by the bang and startled by the old man landing in the vegetable patch with smoke coming from his robes.

Looking out of his now, blackened spectacles the old man staggered around for a moment then patted himself down and made his way back inside the cottage. Even though Bob was in a bad situation himself, he couldn't help but chuckle as he watched. He could see the man was now standing gazing at a floating, rotating, clear, effervescent, orb.

'My goodness,' the old man declared out loud, 'it's finally worked. By Jove! Wolfstun you are a genius.'

He then started doing a little dance, whilst clapping his hands in the air. Jigging his way over to the oscillating orb, he gave it a gentle nudge with his elbow. SCHLOOP. Instantly he was drawn inside the bubble-like orb. 'Wow,' he shrieked, 'this is it, I've done it. Thank goodness.'

Bob realised in an instant that Wolfstun was a Wuzard and obviously a clever one at that.

Sitting down gently in the shining interior of the orb he crossed his legs and made himself comfortable, stretching out his arms in front of him and leaning forward, the orb floated out through the open door, into the bright and beautiful warm afternoon.

Raising his arms above his head, it started to rise upwards, drifting slowly over the rusty red roof and through the purple smoke coming out of the chimney pot, climbing right up to the top of the canopy of the trees.

'My, my,' thought Wolfstun, what a wonderful sight as he floated around in this new orb.

Passing over a clump of fir trees he spotted something catching the light, just by a fallen tree trunk.

Chapter Fifteen

'Base to Bumble, base to Bumble, come in.'

Jack listened intently to what Bumble had to say and, in a calm voice, told him not to panic and to sit tight until he got there.

Jack sprang into action. He ran downstairs, out of the door and whistled. Hoping that the pheasant would hear him and come quickly, he went back inside and grabbed the saddle off its hook.

The pheasant, (who let Jack fly on him, as Jack had once rescued him from a poacher's net) was waiting for him and it wasn't long before they were airborne, flying over the railway line below and following the sparkling silver river. Using the Water Mill as a landmark, the pheasant banked right over Swan Bridge and up Bolton's Lane, flying over the top of Frogden Spinney and across the fields towards Fever Ditch Wood. Jack had been lying flat on the pheasant's back for speed, but sitting up he started to make the bird circle the trees.

To his amazement he saw something else flying in the air, about a hundred meters away. As he got closer he could see it was Wolfstun the Wuzard, in what appeared to be a bubble, zipping to and fro. As he got nearer the Wuzard seemed to be trying to tell him something and was pointing towards the ground, at a big tree that had fallen over.

Jack saw a flash of light reflecting off a dome and realised Wolfstun was trying to tell him something. He gave him the thumbs up.

Jack swooped in low on the pheasant to see what he was up against, he saw the dome surrounded by Blowpines attacking his family inside. He had to formulate a plan to rescue them. Circling around the tops of the trees he knew he had to act fast.

Wolfstun in the orb had drawn level with him so they were flying side by side. Suddenly and without any notice, Wolfstun jumped out of the bubble and had landed in a tree top.

'Steady boy', cried Jack as he tried to keep the pheasant under control. The pheasant wasn't used to people landing in trees next to him.

Jack couldn't understand what had made the Wuzard jump into the tree. The bubble was still there, suspended in the sky, but then Wolfstun waved his arm and it was as if he was in control of the bubble, giving it an order.

He pointed down to where the Steeplers, Harry and Sam were under attack and the weirdest thing happened.

The orb floated down to the nasty Blowpines and one by one, SCHLOOP, sucked them up, all fifteen of them, making them like ping pong balls enclosed in a bouncy castle. Then the orb zoomed off at great speed, until it disappeared from sight.

Jack threw the rope from his rucksack to Wolfstun, who caught one end, tied it to a branch and dropped the other end to the ground. Muttering something, the rope turned ridged and he started to climb down.

Jack landed the pheasant and waited for Wolfstun to reach the ground. He went over to shake Wolfstuns hand and thanked him for his help.

They made their way over to the now very relieved Steeplers and there was a lot of back slapping and big smiles of relief all round.

Chapter Sixteen

Wolfstun shook Sam's hand and introduced himself to everyone who didn't already know him. Buster told Jack what had happened to Bob.

This upset Wolfstun because he had no idea that Bob had been hanging there, so close to his potion house and in desperate need of rescuing.

He volunteered to help them in any way he could to make amends. Jack unsaddled the pheasant and sent it on its way, whilst the rest of them gathered their belongings and set off again. Buster made sure the magic crystal was safely stowed away and felt so relieved that Jack was now with them on their quest. They ventured deeper into the wood, working their way through the undergrowth, and the further they went, the more humid and darker it got.

They stopped now and then for a quick rest and a drink, and after what seemed like ages they came to the potion house by Kingdoms Pool.

Tiff had spotted the smoke through the trees first and was wondering why it was purple and, why was someone having a fire on such a hot and humid day. Joey using his binoculars couldn't believe what he saw.

Bob was dangling from the branch of a tree, all bound up, with just a glimpse of his red checked shirt and boots.

'Come on lads, I can see Bob, we've got to rescue him,' he shouted.

He led them across the large clearing through the tall grass. When they reached Bob, Joey shouted,

'Bob, are you alright mate?'

The Steeple People

'Oh, Joey, thank heavens, I'd nearly given up hope, I'm so glad you're here because I really, really need the loo. I've never been so happy to hear your voice.'

'OK, hold on a little longer mate, we'll soon have you down.'

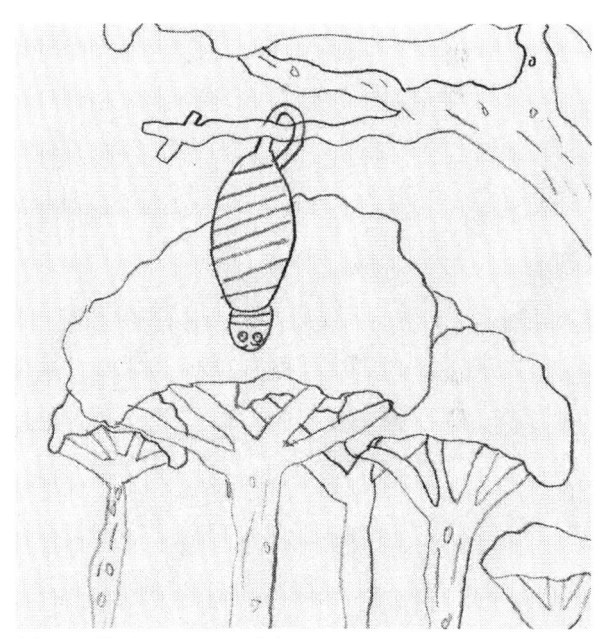

Liam Salter age 11

Bumble gave the boys a bunk up to the first branch of the tree. Climbing slowly, they finally reached the branch where Bob was dangling in the cocoon of the Spiderfly web.

Bumble began pacing the ground below, wringing his hands, as he watched as the boys securing the rope around the branch. Every now and then he would shout up a reassuring word to give them encouragement.

Once Tiff and Joey reached Bob, the first thing they did was to make the hole around his face bigger so that he could speak and breathe more easily. Working with their nimble fingers they began to ease the webbing off his body, not noticing the fine threads attached to the cocoon.

Bob was so relieved that he'd been found and could feel the webbing getting looser by the minute.

Once he was free, and they'd waited for the pins and needles to go from his arms and legs, they slowly started to climb back down the rope.

Tiff in front of Bob and Joey behind him in case he got all wobbly again after being in the same position for so long.

Finally they were nearly at the bottom when they all heard it, in the distance, a clicking, whirring sound getting louder and louder.

'Oh no,' Bob cried, 'they're on their way back.'

'Who are?' Joey asked.

'The flippin' Spiderflies, that's who. That was what captured me this morning and it sounds like there's more than one of them this time.'

He was right. A whole swarm of them was heading straight towards them.

The fine strands attached to Bob's cocoon were in fact tripwires to warn the Spiderflies that something was disturbing their quarry. When Joey and Tiff had freed Bob they had in fact alerted the Spiderflies that someone was taking their dinner.

Harry's eyes were wide open and his ears were flicking backwards and forwards while his tail was swishing from side to side.
'Quick, into the potion house, I can see them,' cried Wolfstun, 'it looks like there are hundreds of them.'

They grabbed their equipment, and quickly legged it down the bank towards the safety of Wolfstun's potion house. As they reached the gate, the nasty flying insects caught up with them and started to attack, flying straight at them, jabbing with their venomous spiked bottoms. Barging open the gate and pulling out his spud gun, Bumble managed to hold off several of them by firing at their wings, while Jack tried to stun them by aiming between their eyes.

Wolfstun was flapping his arms about and mumbling some ancient incantation. Suddenly there was a flash and an almighty bang which made the ground shake and the air around them tingle with electricity.

Wolfstun had conjured up a spell that had given them the few seconds they needed to scurry down the path to reach the cottage. What they didn't know was Wolfstun's spells didn't always go to plan and he'd actually been trying to conjure up a thunderstorm over the swarm of Spiderflies, but all they got was a flash and bang.

Bumble and Jack used the opportunity to run for cover. Harry was the last of the group to cross the threshold skidding to a stop with his hooves making a scrapping sound on the slippery tiles of the floor. He snorted in surprise at finding himself inside and in such a small and strange building, but they were all now safely inside. Wolfstun slammed the door shut and shouted to Sam and Jack to move the dresser against the door.

The noise outside was deafening with the sound of hundreds of Spiderfly wings beating together and the sounds of clicking from their mouths. They were all scared, trapped inside and Bob was now desperate for the loo.

'Wolfstun, where's the thunderbox?' he asked.

Wolfstun nodded towards the back of the cottage and Bob rushed off to find it.

Making his way to the back of the room, Wolfstun passed the shelves full of strange bottles, all of them containing different coloured fluids with strange objects floating inside.

He arrived at a row of levers along one windowless wall, each lever had a small plaque above it indicating what it was for," Pool", "Bridge", "Trapdoor", and "Tunnel". Grabbing hold of one of the levers, he pulled it towards him.

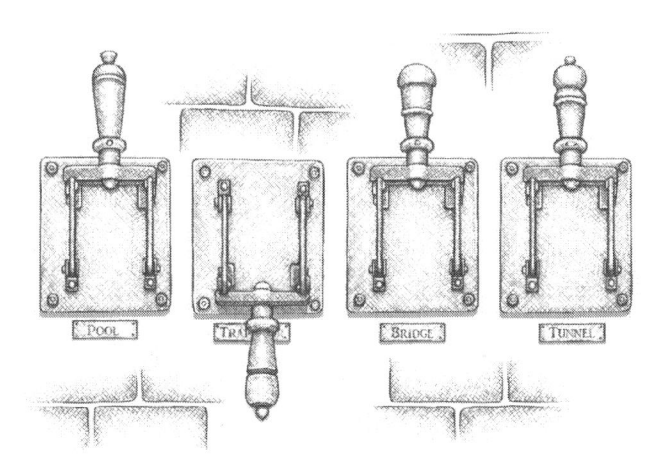

'Ok lads,' he shouted over the noise from outside. 'The only way out is through this trap door. I suggest we get a move on and escape from this place. Now!'

They didn't need to be asked twice, and quickly lined up ready to go down the steps into the gloom below, just as Bob came out of the loo and joined the back of the queue.

'Harry and I will stay here' said Sam. 'We've got you covered this end.'

'Okay then, thanks.' Wolfstun began helping the rest of the Steeplers down through the trapdoor. As he descended he looked over his shoulder and said, 'You know what to do Sam, don't forget, count to thirty and then release the lever.'

'Okay,' Sam said, and once they had all reached the bottom, he pushed the lever back again closing the door in the floor.

Chapter Seventeen

Scampering along the tiny passageway they came to a ladder going up to a small wooden hatch above. Climbing out one by one they found themselves out in the open by Kingdoms Pool, about thirty metres away from the swirling mass of horrible Spiderflies.

'Twenty-eight, twenty-nine, thirty…..' Back at the potion house, Sam finished counting then reached for the lever with "bridge" next to it. He slowly pulled it which made the bridge swing out from the side of the bank to the centre of Kingdoms Pool. He then reached for the fourth lever and pulled that too.

The purple smoke that everyone had been so puzzled about earlier, started to twist and turn into a rope, making an arc from the chimney stack to the centre of the pool. At the same time the water in the pool started to swirl round and round, creating a vortex which spiralled down, like water going down a plug hole. The Steeplers stood and watched in wonder.

The Wuzard was keeping an eye on the Spiderflies attacking the cottage.

The motion of the bridge and the smoke seemed to get the attention of a couple of them. He really didn't want the swarm to turn towards them, so, tapping Jack on the shoulder, he indicated for them to follow him and began running across the bridge. He reached the purple rope, jumped on to it and began sliding down, disappearing into the void below.

Unfortunately, some of the Spiderflies had noticed the movement over at the pool and a few of them started to peel away from the rest and headed straight towards them.

Suddenly there was an almighty crash, followed by the sound of something smashing its way through the undergrowth.

'Oh no! What's that?' cried Joey as he dashed across the bridge, following the rest. Tiff shouted back, 'Just keep running mate, take no notice or we're done for.' He didn't even turn round to look.

Almost immediately they heard a roar and felt the heat of red hot flames going over their heads, towards the incoming Spiderflies. This was instantly followed by another roar, even louder than the first, then they heard the sound of sparks cracking and popping like fireworks.

Neither of them stopped to look, but just kept running. Just before Joey leapt towards the rigid rope, he allowed himself a glance over his shoulder to see Terry the Tygon bursting out from the vegetation, bounding at full speed towards the flying attackers. As Terry levelled with the bridge he could see the last of the Steeplers disappearing into the watery gloom of the spinning pool. Standing up on his hind legs and using his bright red dragon tail to steady himself he let out another burst of deadly flames which singed the wings and webs of the attacking Spiderflies who were almost upon him.

Finally the ugly swarm retreated, having had enough wrath from the striped, fire-breathing Tygon.

After the Steeplers and Wolfstun had disappeared into the vortex and the rope and bridge had returned to their original state, the Spiderflies continued to attack the potion house. Sam quickly mixed up some potions into a powder and threw it on to the fire in the corner of the room.
Flash. Whizz. Whooosh!

Sparks flew everywhere, instantly the smoke turned from purple to acrid dark green, which went up the chimney and swirled round over the top of the little red roof. It did the trick, the Spiderflies did not like it one little bit. One sniff of the pungent smoke fumes and the swarm disappeared as quickly as they'd arrived.

After ten minutes or so, when the smoke had disappeared, Sam shoved the dresser away from the door and gingerly stepped outside. He checked the sky for any lingering Spiderflies and once he was satisfied that they had all gone he gave a sigh of relief. It was over.

Sam led Harry outside and patted him on the neck, 'Well done, old fella, he said. Then with some apprehension he approached Terry and held out his hand as you to greet a dog. He managed to get close enough to stroke the Tygon on his warm but wet nose. 'And the same to you, Terry, without you we would still be in a lot of trouble.'

Poking out his thin lizard like tongue, Terry licked the back of Sam's hand. They both took a step back and bowed their heads to one another in respect. Then Terry turned and slowly padded back into the depths of Fever Ditch Wood.

Sam swung himself up onto Harry and made his way home back through the woods.

Chapter Eighteen

Joey was the last to descend to the bottom of the swirling, spinning tube of muddy water, of Kingdoms Pool, ending up on top of Tiff who'd arrived seconds before. Luckily, all the others had landed safely, probably from all the practice they'd had sliding down the fireman's pole back at the Steeple.

The water above them very slowly stopped rotating and the rope retracted upwards through the diminishing hole. They were now under the water, but inside the pool. They realised there was a seal covering them, like when you go to the aquarium and walk through the glass tunnels.

With a sigh of relief the little chaps sat down on the dusty, rocky floor and just gazed at each other. They were wiped out. It was Buster who spoke first.

'And what the Dickens was all that about?'

'Did you see that Tygon that turned up at the end?' said Jack. 'He was really scary, but it looked as if he was trying to help us. That or he really doesn't like Spiderflies either.'

'I'm pretty sure that was Terry.' Joey said, and they all agreed except Jack who looked puzzled.

'Eh? Terry? Who's Terry?'

'It's a long story I'll tell you later Jack, but one thing is certain, I never want to go to that place ever again.' Bumble replied.

They all nodded in agreement, with the exception of Wolfstun, who of course, lives there.

Once their eyes got used to the dark, they began to notice there were doors in the walls of the room they were in, which appeared to be a horseshoe shaped hall. The only light came from the murky water above.

Each door had a brass plaque with an inscription on it and an ornate key in a glass box beside it. Using his torch, Bob shone the light on each of the plaques, going from one to another, and Joey read out the inscriptions.

'Kingdom of the South Seas, Kingdom of Ghosts, Kingdom of Dreams. I wonder what all that means,' he said scratching his head.

'Ah,' the Wuzard gave a little cough, 'I can enlighten you on this, gentlemen. We have now entered the Assembly Hall of Journey. Here you can enter through those doors into the Kingdoms inscribed on the plaque. They are all different and you can choose the one you want to go into.'

Joey sighed. 'I think we've had quite enough adventure for one day, thank you Wolfstun.'

The old man carried on, ignoring him. 'To enter the weird and wonderful worlds you have to solve the riddle hidden behind the brass plaques. Then you must chalk your answer on the blackboard you'll find by each door in a box. If you show it to the spyhole and have answered correctly you may then retrieve the key from the box and the door to that Kingdom can be opened.'

'Golly, this place is awesome lads,' Jack said smiling broadly. 'Can you imagine the adventures you and the girls could have through those I suppose you would call them, portals?'

'Oh yes,' Tiff scoffed. 'Just one small problem Dad.'

'What's that then son?'

'Um, getting here and back without being set upon, shot at, stung, or tied up.'

Wolfstun was chuckling to himself. 'Let me help you there young man. Right, now look behind you and you will see another door set apart from the others.' They all looked in the direction that he was pointing. 'Go and see what it says on that door lad, go on.'

Tiff went over and looked at the words etched on the brass plaque and read them aloud.

'Curley Castle. This way. Exit. Hmmm. Oh I see, an escape route.'

'Yes, there is a way out from here, and if you choose it, there is a way back in too through a long winding tunnel,' Wolfstun explained.

'That's brilliant. You mean we could come and go as we please?' Tiff asked. The Wuzard nodded.

'That's amazing, Aunt Lucy and I were born in Curley Castle, and we never knew. Well blow me down,' said Jack. 'Right, come

The Steeple People

on you lot, let's have a go at one of these riddles then? Tiff, get on my shoulders so you can read it.' How about the first one, the Kingdom of the South Seas?' he said with a sparkle in his eye.

'Just a little look then,' said Bob. 'Remember, I haven't eaten all day and I don't want to miss my tea, and my bottom don't half throb from that sting.'

Jack bent his head down so Tiff could sit on his shoulders and then he stood up straight. Tiff was now at the right height to read the plaque.

'OK,' Jack replied, positioning himself so Tiff could read the plaque more easily.

'We'll have a quick peek and then we'll head back to the old homestead, I promise.'

Lifting the plaque up on its hinges, Tiff read the inscription on the reverse.

'What can you feel but you cannot touch? What can you hear but cannot see? Hmmm, that's a hard one.'

'Anybody got any ideas?' asked Jack looking round at them all.

After scratching their heads for a few minutes, Buster said, 'How about breath?' You can't see that, or touch it.'

'Oh well done, mate, that's a good one. Joe reached over and opened the box, passing the board and chalk to Tiff.'

Writing "Breath" on the black surface, Tiff turned the blackboard to face the spyhole in the front of the door, where an eye suddenly appeared.

After a few seconds the eye disappeared and returned to being a spyhole. Nothing happened.

'Well, that can't be right then can it?' said Jack. 'Anyone got any more ideas?'

'Oh, I know why it's wrong,' said Bob, 'you can see your breath on a cold winter's morning.'

'Of course you can,' said Jack, and they all nodded in agreement.

'Well, let's try something similar then. How about wind? Give that a try,' said Bob and with that his tummy rumbled.

Tiff rubbed out, "breath" and wrote "wind" on the little blackboard instead. Turning it to the spyhole, the eye appeared again. It glanced at the blackboard and then disappeared. This time, however, they heard a click come from the glass box containing the key.

'Yeah,' they cried.
'Well done, Bob,' said Jack, 'go on Tiff grab the key and open the door.'

Nervously Tiff took hold of the key and placing it into the lock he turned it. Hearing a dull thud, he knew it had worked so he gave the door a slight push, it opened slowly with a loud creaking sound.

Chapter Nineteen

A warm breeze wafted out from the open door and the smell of the sea and hot beach came with it. The little fellows peered around the big wooden door and an orange glow shone onto their tired faces.

Stepping through and entering into this new kingdom they found themselves on a balcony, with a flight of steps off to the right descending down onto a beach. They could see other flights of steps coming down from other balconies. But there was something very odd about everything.

For a start the sand on the beach was turquoise blue. The sea was daffodil yellow and the sky was pea green. The moon, which was a deep red, and the silver glistening sun were in the sky at the same time. They could hear bells chiming in the gentle warm air and below they could see what looked like pirate boats but they were floating in the sky and not in the sea.

On the blue beach a fluorescent green fire flickered, with hippo-type creatures dancing around it chanting some words and making sounds they didn't understand.

Pulling gently on Jack's shirt, Joey whispered in his ear, 'Can we go home please Dad? It's all getting a bit too much for me and I don't think Bob looks very well at all.'

In fact after he'd given the answer to the riddle, poor old Bob had begun to take a turn for the worse. He'd followed them into the strange kingdom, but then found he couldn't walk very well and kept stumbling around. All at once he became short of breath, then just as he'd spotted the hippos, he blacked out, exactly like earlier after he'd been stung, and fell to the floor with a thump.

'Oh no, look at Bob, he's passed out,' cried Tiff, as he dashed over and knelt down beside him, putting his hand under Bob's head, 'He looks pretty bad, Dad.' He brushed the dust from Bob's face and moved his hair out of his eyes.

'Move over a bit son, let me take a look at him'. Jack placed his ear next to Bob's mouth to see if he was breathing, which he was, only just. 'Hmmm doesn't look good, you're right he's out cold'. Standing up, Jack turned to Buster and told him to get the Rhombus Spectrum box out of his rucksack so they could use it.

Placing it down on the dusty floor, Jack stood back and recited the magic words to activate it 'Rhombus Spectrum' he said in a clear and crisp voice but nothing happened. 'That's funny,' he thought to himself. Clearing his throat he repeated,

'Rhombus Spectrum'. Again nothing happened.

'What's wrong Dad?' asked Joey looking concerned.
'I don't know son.' Jack was scratching his head. 'Maybe it needs time to charge back up or something?'

'You could be right Jack,' Bumble said, joining in. 'I noticed that by the time we had finished using it in the woods, it wasn't as bright as it was when we first used it.' Bumble was beginning to panic now.

Jack picked up the box and started to inspect it, he noticed the embossed elephant on the lid of the casket was loose. Lifting it up with his thumbnail he saw some very tiny words written beneath.

The power within will keep you safe, come what may
But only if each power is used but twice a day

'So, that's it,' looking up he said, 'we've used up all its energy for today. We'll have to come up with another plan.'

Looking at Wolfstun he asked, 'Have you got any potions we can use?'

Pushing up the brim of his hat with his staff, the Wuzard replied, 'I can do a few things very well but, unfortunately, anything to do with medicine has always been a bit hit and miss for me I'm afraid. I once tried to mend the leg of a Panthicorn, a black wild cat with a horn on its head, but alas, after my incantation, all its teeth fell out.'

'Oh dear, I think we need to think fast, I'm worried about Bob now, any other ideas? Anyone?' said Jack.

'One of these doors might just be able to help,' Wolfstun said.
'OK, which one?' Said Jack stepping towards the Wuzard.
'Which one? Hmmmm, something to do with Health and something, what was it now,' he was deep in thought scratching his hairy chin. 'I can't remember exactly, we'll just have to check them all again.'

So with that, they split up and started checking the doors, except Bumble who stayed next to Bob. There were loads of them which they hadn't noticed before. The Kingdom of Chance, The Kingdom of Ice, and finally they came to the last door in the half circled hall, and this one had chalk writing over the top of the original name.

The Steeple People

The Kingdom of Elf and Booty. Buster was in front of the door, 'I wonder what that means?' he thought. 'Wolfstun,' he called. 'Come and see this.'

When Wolfstun saw it, he smiled and said, 'Them Skimpies have been at it again.'
'Skimpies?' asked Tiff, 'what are Skimpies?'

Wolfstun rubbed the chalk off and revealed the words underneath.

'Skimpies are very naughty elves they are always up to no good, playing tricks, and it would appear they have been to work here. Look,' he said pointing to the plaque. The Kingdom of Health and Beauty it read.

Bobby Days

Everyone else had joined them now, he turned to the rest of the gang, 'Skimpies work for pirates, who protect them and look after their needs, while the pirates use the Skimpies for carrying and hiding their treasure which they call booty. So it seems that behind this door, could be help available for Bob but it could also be dangerous because of the pirates. What do you think? Shall we risk it?'

'I don't think we've got a choice, Bob's getting weaker by the minute and the longer we wait the worse he'll be,' said Buster.

'Right,' said Jack, 'Come on, let's get in there and see if there is anything or anybody who can help us, but first we have to answer this bloomin' riddle.'

Wolfstun did the honours and read the riddle aloud.

'What is as big as a mountain but weighs nothing.'

'Come on lads, let's put our thinking caps on and work it out,' said Buster.

Time ticked by and no-one had the slighted idea, then suddenly, Tiff blurted out, 'Hold on. Hold on. I think I've got it.' He started pacing in a circle, 'you know that cracker we had in the Christmas hamper?'

'Yes,' they all replied.

'Well, there was a motto in it and, if I recall, it was pretty much the same question.'

'So what was it Bruv?' asked Joey.

'Oh dear, what was it? Hmmmmm….that's it, it was shadow,' said Tiff.

'Shadow,' of course, said Jack. 'It can be as big as you like but weigh nothing. OK, quick, Wolfstun write it on the blackboard and show it to the weird eye.'

Wolfstun did what he was told and held up the blackboard to the eye. A few seconds later, CLICK. The little glass box opened and with a sigh of relief he picked up the key and turned it in the lock.

Chapter Twenty

Bob was laid on the ground, looking as though he was fast asleep but his tummy was now protruding from his shirt. Bumble picked him up underneath his arms and Buster grabbed hold of his legs. Bob didn't even stir. Slowly they carried Bob over to the door from where they could hear seagulls.

Brushing past them with his long tattered coat flowing behind him, Wolfstun put his shoulder squarely to the door, and giving it a really good shove the door fully opened, allowing them to enter into this new kingdom.

'WOW,' whispered Joey as he looked up at the cliffs around them, 'it looks a bit like Cornwall doesn't it Tiff?'

The little group slowly edged forward. Shadowing his eyes from the sun, Joey could see a huge person in front of him, wearing a tricorn hat and a red coat with braided gold piping on the collars and cuffs.

Sporting a bright red beard the man was clutching a curved cutlass in his enormous hands on which he had a gold ring on every finger. He was staring at them.

The Steeple People

They all stopped and Wolfstun cleared his throat, and spoke in a soft voice.

'Let me introduce you to my dear friend, and fellow Wuzard, Captain Escanius Whistlemist. Skipper of the good ship, Moon Surfer, the finest craft on these three seas.'

And with that Wolfstun took off his hat and bowed.
 'We've been on many adventure together haven't we Scany?' he said looking at his friend.
 'Oh AHH... we 'ave,'Escanius replied in a pirate like voice. 'Never knowin' where we be goin' or if we'd be coming back again. That was us, weren't it Wolfie?' He grabbed his friend and gave him a huge bear hug.
 Wriggling free, Wolfstun took the Captain and in hushed tones started a conversation with him out of earshot of the

Steeplers. A few nods later, the pirate strode back to the group.

'I 'ear one of you's, in a bit of bovver? Righto, never let it be said that Captain Whistlemist is not a kind and helpful gentleman. Do you think you can make it down the beach? We need to get this fellow onto my ship that be anchored out in that peagreen sparkling sea? I've got a boat to row the last bit, but it could be a tricky journey with an invalid.'

Chapter Twenty One

The raggle-taggle little crowd carried Bob on to the beach and into Captain Whistlemist's boat and true to his word he'd rowed them out to his ship. They managed to get the still unconscious Bob onto the poopdeck, then through two swinging doors and then down steps to the Captain's cabin. They laid him on his side in the Captain's bed.

Hiding behind the curtains, were some strange little elf-like creatures, with spikey hair of different colours (like tabby cats) and long, thin noses. Their ears were banjo shaped with the neck part, sticking up. They didn't have mouths but something that resembled a party blower where the paper bit unwinds when you blow. They were all wearing striped all-in-one suits, like a onesie and they all had strange webbed feet. Joey thought they were a bit odd to say the least but they were not scary and it appeared they were loyal to Captain Whistlemist. These were the Skimpies

After they had laid Bob on the bed, one of the Skimpies approached him and gently placed his hand on Bob's back. Tenderly rubbing it he turned to the rest of the Skimpies and in a shrill trumpet like noise, seemed to give orders to the rest of the group.

Wolfstun and the Steeplers were relieved that the Skimpies seemed to know what to do.

Two of the Skimpies darted from the room and Tiff and Joey followed them outside onto the deck to watch. The two strange creatures started to climb the mast, one with a stoppered bottle and one with a lollipop.

Tiff, Joey, and now the rest of the Steeplers, watched as they reached the top and then seemed to be enticing something from the crow's nest. Joey got out his binoculars and said in disbelief,

'Uh, Buster, did you say Decapus were friendly creatures? I think that's what's up there in the crow's nest.'

'I'm not sure really Joey, as I've never come across one before but I think I've heard that they are pretty OK unless you were to frighten one. Give me a look through the binoculars lad.'

One Skimpie was distracting the Decapus who seemed quite interested in the lollipop and the other was collecting its ink in the bottle. Suddenly, the Decapus gave a flick of one of his tentacles, which sent both the small spiky creatures flying through the air.

There was a collective gasp from the crowd below. The Skimpies didn't seem at all bothered. Whilst flying through the air the one with the bottle put the stopper in it and the other one, realising he still had a lollipop in his hand, smiled and started to lick it.

They both landed in a sail, which then catapulted them all the way back to the deck, where they landed on their feet and started immediately running back towards the cabin.

The rest of the group, who had been watching this, all stood still with their mouths open, then gathered themselves together and followed them below decks.

The Skimpie passed over the bottle to the one that was still rubbing Bob's back. He trumpeted some words to the rest of the funny little creatures and they started to take Bob's boots and socks off and another one went to fetch a brush. The head Skimpie then started to paint Bob's feet with the ink. When he'd finished, they all seemed to be in a hurry to leave the room.

'I think we should follow their lead and get out of the room,' said Wolfstun.

Everybody looked at each other blankly and then they all tried to scramble out of the door at the same time. Just as the last of the Steeplers left the room, three Skimpies ran to the windows and opened them up as wide as they could, then slammed the door as they exited. Standing on the poopdeck, they all waited.

The Steeplers were very anxious as none of them knew what was supposed to be happening.

Suddenly there was a rumbling sound, then the sound of gurgling and then the loudest PAAARRRRPPPP you've ever heard came from the cabin below. Followed by two more PARPS and then a long silence and one long last Peeeaaarrrpp.

The first sound heard over the squawking seagulls was Wolfstun chuckling and then Buster started chuckling too, followed by Bumble and the boys. That then turned into a laugh, then a belly laugh and then they were falling around the deck, clutching their sides with tears rolling down their cheeks.

'Wind, it was wind,' Bumble cried out. 'The poor old boy was full of wind.' Steadying himself against some ropes he turned to Buster. 'That Spiderfly sting must make you fill up with gas and by the look of it, the only antidote is Decapus ink.'

'Well blow me down,' said Buster, which made them all start laughing again.

Once they had gathered themselves together and wiped the tears of laughter from their cheeks they crept down to the cabin. Slowly opening the door, they saw Bob sitting up in the bed with a grin of satisfaction on his face.

'Oh, I feel so much better now, 'he said.

Chapter Twenty Two

Captain Escanius Whistlemist, stood proudly on the bow of his magnificent old galleon and was looking directly below at the reflection of the figurehead in the sparkling water. It was a seahorse painted post box red tinged with gold, and it stood out against the aquamarine waters of the beautiful little bay.

Turning around to face his crew and the intrepid bunch of very likeable small travellers and his old friend Wolfstun, he boomed out in his distinct Cornish accent.

'Ahoy there, I'll be 'avin' your attention, if 'e don't mind. It's so good to see me old Wuzarding friend here this afternoon and I was very pleased to be of assistance today.'

The Skimpies all clapped their hands in agreement.

Bobby Days

'So I've decided to 'av a party to celebrate our friendship and being able to help one of your new found friends.' With that they all applauded and gave a couple of whoop –whoops. 'Now without further ado, let's be 'avin a PARTY!'

What a brilliant time they all had. Duncan the Decapus was lured from the crow's nest with a handful of lollipops and they put him front of a set of old empty gunpowder kegs and he started drumming a beat with all his ten tentacles. The Skimpies joined in playing their banjo ears in time to the rhythm. The Captain and Wolfstun started doing a jig and not long after everyone joined in. The Skimpies brought out food but not proper food, just sweets, loads of them, more lollipops, sherbet dib dabs and jelly beans. Joey and Tiff nearly made themselves sick .

'Now that's what I call a party,' Bumble said. After they thanked the Skimpies, they waved goodbye as Captain Whistlemist rowed them back to the shore.

Wolfstun and the Captain made promises to meet up again soon and then the group made its way back through the big heavy door and into the round chamber.

'They should call that the Kingdom of Cornwall,' Joey said as he slapped his bother on the back.

Tiff turned to his Dad and said 'Can we go home now please, Dad?'

'Of course, son, yes of course we can.'

They were all very tired and it had been an extremely long day. Making their way along the passage towards Curley Castle, for the first time that day no-one spoke.

Once they reached the end of the tunnel, the Steeplers pushed open a big iron gate and stepped outside. They drew in the sweet scent of the fresh air, deep into their lungs.

'Well then boys, I think we ought to head back home,' said Jack.

Wolfstun, clapped his hands twice and out of nowhere, the bubble, now empty of its cargo of Blowpines, arrived.

'Where did they go?' asked Jack.

'Far, far away,' Wolfstun chuckled, 'they won't be bothering us again.'

And with that he elbowed the shimmering orb and they were sucked in, one and all. SCHLOOP. It took no time to arrive back at the Grange. Bidding the very wise Wolfstun farewell, they waved him off in his bubble-like orb.

Chapter Twenty Three

Once home they realised they were hungry and decided that they would like a barbecue feast. So they all went outside under the canopy stretched between the villas in the field. Jack fired up the barbecue and Mam provided them all with mouth-watering salads with plenty of burgers and sausages. After stuffing their faces, they decided to put their feet up, so lit some candles, which looked like fire flies dotted around them.

    Buster turned to Jack. 'When do the girls get back?' he asked 'It seems ages since they went.'

    'Tomorrow lunchtime. I hope they've had a lovely time of it in Cornwall.'

    'Well I hope they bring us back some pasties,' said Tiff, 'I do love a good Cornish pasty.'

Everyone chuckled. The boys sang some songs and Buster accompanied them on his ukulele. They were still buzzing with excitement and would not have been able to sleep after everything they had been through that day, so Mam thought it better to let them stay up a bit later and relax before getting them all to go to bed. She and Jack were sitting on some straw bales having a nice cup of cocoa and silently she thanked her lucky stars that all the family had returned in one piece.

The next morning Buster, Bumble and Jack rose very early. The grass was sparkling with dew and a warm morning sun was rising over the hills. They went off to retrieve the balloon boats and flew them back home ready for the journey that afternoon to Combe Feast Fair. Bob was having his second breakfast of the morning. The girls had also arrived back from their holiday and couldn't wait to tell everyone what they'd been up to.

That afternoon, filling the balloons to full capacity, they all climbed on board, including Mam who really doesn't like flying much.

Buster wound up the elastic bands with the lollipop propeller, then let go and leapt into the basket. They threw out some stones that were weighing them down and slowly the boats started to rise.

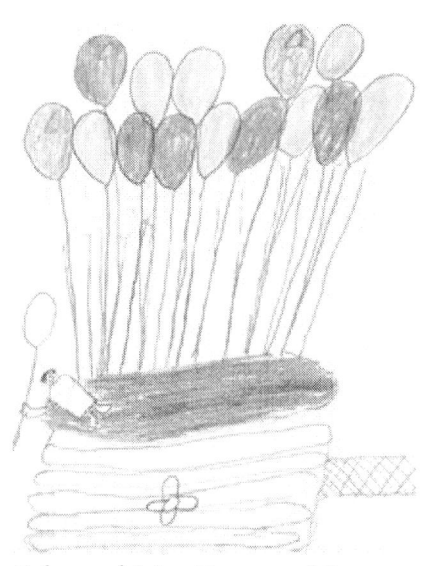

Edward Martin age 11

Floating gradually at first, and then catching the wind, they flew in the direction of the Combe Feast. They were all talking about the weird creatures they'd seen

'Wasn't it amazing, Buster?' said Joey.

'Yes Joey,' Buster replied, although amazing wasn't quite the word he would have used.

'Hey up, we're nearly there,' cried Tiff, who was half hanging out of the basket, 'I can't wait to see if they still have the nelly burgers this year.'

Flying just over the tops of the fairground's brightly coloured tents they were all so excited.

'Look, there's Graham Harpoon, the drummer from Freefall, with his wife, Sue, having a drink, and see there's old Davey boy, leading his ponies, Dylan and Bramble, for the young children to ride.' Buster was pointing out everything excitedly.

Landing in the field next to the fair, behind the stone wall, the boys leapt out and ran towards the stalls. They helped each other over the stone wall and then ran towards the dodgem cars. Buster secured the airships with a big stone and made his way over to have a look round too.

Jack and Mam took a much more leisurely pace and ducked under the gate of the field before heading towards the Waltzers.

Mam loved the Waltzers, they were her favourite.

'Well, Mam,' Jack said quietly, while putting his arm through hers and kissing her on the cheek, 'I suppose all's well that ends well.'

She smiled and whispered back, 'I love you Jack Steeple.' Then Jack lifted her up onto the ride and jumped on beside her.

The Steeple People

The end
Until the next time, happy holiday's to you all.

Printed in Poland
by Amazon Fulfillment
Poland Sp. z o.o., Wrocław